D0099617

For every little girl who is becoming a big girl.
I like you just the way you are.
Shine, girl, shine!

—V.B.-N.

THIS IS A BORZOI BOOK PUBLISHED BY ALFRED A. KNOPF

Copyright © 2020 by Vanessa Brantley-Newton

All rights reserved. Published in the United States by Alfred A. Knopf,
an imprint of Random House Children's Books, a division of Penguin Random House LLC, New York.

Knopf, Borzoi Books, and the colophon are registered trademarks of Penguin Random House LLC.

Visit us on the Web! rhcbooks.com

Educators and librarians, for a variety of teaching tools, visit us at RHTeachersLibrarians.com

Library of Congress Cataloging-in-Publication Data is available upon request.
ISBN 978-0-525-58209-0 (trade) — ISBN 978-0-525-58210-6 (lib. bdg.) — ISBN 978-0-525-58211-3 (ebook)

The text of this book is set in 16-point Colby Narrow Regular.
The illustrations were created using acrylic paint, gouache, charcoal, pencil,
oil pastels, handmade and collage papers, and lots of magic.

Book design by Nicole de las Heras

MANUFACTURED IN CHINA
January 2020
10 9 8 7 6 5 4 3 2 1

First Edition

Just Like Me

Vanessa Brantley-Newton

Alfred A. Knopf
New York

I Am a Canvas

I am a canvas

being painted on

by the words of my family

friends

and community

Sometimes the words are painted with blacks and grays

that leave me feeling confused

Other times the palette is filled with blues

that make me want to scream

and holler

in a bluesy kind of way

"I am not feeling it today!"

And then there are days

when pinks and purples

flow over my canvas

like the sky and give me hope

for a different tomorrow

And then there are the paints that I get to choose

Greens, yellows, oranges, and blues

The Day I Decided to Become Sunshine

The day I decided to become sunshine
in my own world
everything changed
I decided to shine my little light
into the darkest corners
of my community
I decided to be a light
by holding a door
open for others to come through

And to shine the light
of kindness into my every move
The day I decided to become sunshine
I felt like I could change the world

Warrior

I am a warrior
willing to fight the good fight
Respectfully
with humanity
and lovingly

with all the kindness inside of me
In my own unique way
I am a warrior
willing to fight the good fight
of love

All in Together Girls

How do you like American girls?
Every culture
Every race
Every color
Every face

We all belong to the human race
If we view each other with amazing grace
our America would be such a great place

I Love My Body

I love my body
with all of its flaws
Missing teeth
and crazy hair
Ashy knees
and elbows
Long lanky legs
that run wobbly
I love these freckles
that run along my cheeks
and my neck
and upper arms
like maps
telling me who I am
It is much more than telling me
that I am beautiful
It is allowing me
to be the me
that I'm supposed to be

Pimples

This pimple has invited itself
to my perfect picture day
And all I really want
is for it to go away
And find some other lovely
face to make its home upon
There's a pesky pimple on my face
and I just want it gone

Summer Loves

I love
hot summer days
with open fire hydrants
on street corners
and bodegas filled with
dill pickles and red hots

I love
sitting on the stoop
watching the B boys and girls

dance and
Nae Nae
I can Nae Nae too

I love
the sound of the ice cream truck
coming down the block
bringing cool sweet relief from the heat
and moving to the sound
of a hip-hop beat

Sundress Blues

My sundress and I
are no longer friends
It ended
when the wind began
blowing my dress
here and there

and showing off
my underwear
Well . . .
at least they were cute

City and

I am a city girl
longing to be a country girl
climbing trees and picking butter beans
and learning Gullah ways
Drinking sweet tea and watching the sun
    set on soft sandy dirt roads
and the gentle sound of crickets
I am a city girl
longing to be a country one

Country Dreams

I am a country girl
longing to be a city girl
chasing bright lights and crowded streets
and dirty water dogs
And learning that fast city talk
and chasing ice cream trucks
and watching the sun set from fire escapes
I am a country girl
longing to be a city one

Waiting for Friends

I brought an extra sandwich
and a big bag of kisses
and my bright hopes
of making a friend today

Explorer

I am an explorer
going places that I've never
    even heard of
or seen with my eyes
But I feel in my heart
I am going places

And through daydreams
and night dreams
flying high in the sky
I am an explorer
exploring possibilities

Weird

I love me weird and strange

I love my peanut butter sandwiches with jelly beans

I love a good Coca-Cola with peanuts inside

I love to sit behind the living room drapes reading my books

and talking to invisible friends about wild adventures

I love the sound of double-Dutchers on street corners

the tap-tap-tapping of their feet

I love the smell of Mama's black coffee and the strong flavor when I steal a sip

I love the sound of creaky doors and squeaky floors

and I love a good scare

I love my friends

who are different from me

'cause that's what a friend is supposed to be

Some are funny

some are cute

All are brilliant

and sweet

But they are them

and I am me

And if you're weird

then you have a friend in me

Weird
girls rule!!

You

If you were a flower
I'd pick you
to go inside of
a beautiful bouquet
and that would make
my day

Negotiator

I am a negotiator

Can I stay up tonight?

I am a negotiator

I can break up a fight and make things right

So can I stay up tonight?

Little Sister

I am a little sister
but I want to be a big sister
so that I can wear high-heel shoes
and sparkly leggings
and makeup
and have a cell phone
and talk to my friends
But then I wouldn't get the lap time
or the cuddles
and bedtime stories
I'll pass on being a big sister for now

Of Bullies and Monsters

Bullies
monsters
dragons
and goons

try to scare
me with gloom
and doom

But I just
pull out my dustpan
and broom
and sweep them
away
I'm brave today
Yay!

Fearless
focused
and fierce
as I can be
Look out, world,
I hope you're
ready for me

Door Buster

Wasn't invited to the party
Wasn't invited to play
Wasn't invited to be a part
But y'all gonna want me one day

I can't promise that I'll be here
the next time you come around
So why don't you just open the door
'cause next time I'm kicking it down

Cool Like That

I bip I bop

I hip I hop

I play and slay

these drums

all day

I blat and bap

those snares I tap

while rappers rap

'cause I'm cool

like that

Girl Fight

Girl fight
Girl fight
Girls fighting for their rights
to be heard
Voices raised high
Girls fighting for
a piece of the pie

Girls fighting for independence
and civil rights
Won't you hear our plight
and see our marching feet
We will fight for what we believe

Memawh's Wisdom

Instructions in her voice
about making right choices
Carrots over candy
Water instead of soda
A book instead of
playing video games
Face-to-face conversations
instead of texting
Because you can't see someone's soul
in a text
And I hear her words
as wrinkled hands gently cup my face
All we have is this time, baby girl
Making memories
that don't need to be backed up
or downloaded,
and being present

Instructions in her voice
Baby girl,
make the right choice
Carrots over candy
and keep the Good Book handy
Watch what you say
and don't forget to pray
You'll be a great lady someday
if from these instructions
you do not stray

A Wish for Daddy

He brings her to school
and then picks her up
He kisses her forehead
and gives her a big hug
She dances on his feet
and he tells her she's sweet
I wish I had a daddy
That would be so neat

Feelings

Bright as
a lightning bug
busy as a bee
carefree as a butterfly
flying happily
Fresh as a daisy
fluffy as a cloud
loud as a lion
roaring in a crowd

Quiet as a mouse
cranky as a bear
angry as a hornet
zooming through the air
All of these feelings
live inside of me
All of them are who I am . . .
Are you feeling me?

I Am

I am a song
longing to be sung

I am the shine
belonging to the sun

I am the sweetness
in the breeze

I am the roots of
the big oak tree

I am the fish
swimming in the sea

Results of ancestors'
prayers to be free

Shy

I am shy

but there is a big
voice deep inside

it's wild and free
and it's pushing me

to be bold and open
to making new friends

I cast all my cares
into the wind

I open my heart
and my mouth soon follows

I think good thoughts
and then I swallow

and eke out the
smallest, but kindest, "Hello!"

brave thing to do
I'm not shy today

Gumbo Me

I am gumbo
a little bit of everything
and everyone
mixed all together
to make me
special

My Crown

My hair is
magical
unique and free
It's wild and crazy
Just like me

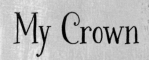

Paper Chains

Like a paper chain
made of every single
color
we link up to
level up
and aspire to go

higher and higher
pulling each other up
so that she can be
a powerful link in our paper chain
encouraging each other to be
gentle yet strong

loving and kind
each one reaching out
until our link crosses this world
like the change
we long to see
We can't do it until everyone joins

until all are invited
Won't you be a link in our
paper chain for change?